R

Maggie Moore and Paula Knight

W
FRANKLIN WATTS

Once upon a time there was a little girl called Red Riding Hood.

Little Red Riding Hood lived with her parents in a little thatch-roofed cottage in the forest.

One day her mother said, "Your
grandmother is ill. I have baked
her a cake."
Red Riding Hood jumped up and said,
"Poor Grandmother, I'll go immediately."

Grandmother lived on the other side of the forest at the end of a long, dark road.

"Go straight there," said her mother. "Do not stop or talk to anyone."

"Don't worry," smiled Little Red Riding Hood, "I'll be careful."

In the forest, near the road, lived the
Big Bad Wolf! He liked to watch
who walked through
the forest.

Little Red Riding Hood saw beautiful flowers as she walked along the dark road. "Grandmother loves flowers," she thought to herself. "I'll take some to cheer her up."

The Big Bad Wolf watched as Little Red
Riding Hood picked the flowers.
"Mmm!" he thought, "A delicious
little girl."
He crept quietly behind her, ready
to pounce.

But Little Red Riding Hood heard
the crackling of twigs behind her
and swiftly turned round.
Quickly the Big Bad Wolf put on
a big smile.
"Hello, little girl," he said. "Where
are you going?"

"I'm taking cake and flowers to my grandmother. She is poorly and they will cheer her up," replied Little Red Riding Hood.

The Big Bad Wolf smiled to himself. "Grandmother is on her own and I'm going to eat her up!"

He raced through the forest to Grandmother's cottage and pounded on the door.

"Who's there?" demanded
Grandmother.
"It's me, Little Red Riding Hood,"
he growled.

"That doesn't sound like Little Red Riding Hood," thought Grandmother and she hid herself in a cupboard.

The Big Bad Wolf tumbled into the cottage and looked for Grandmother. "She's gone," he grumbled, "but Little Red Riding Hood is coming soon. I know what I'll do."

15

He found a nightgown and cap, put them on, jumped into bed and snuggled under the covers.

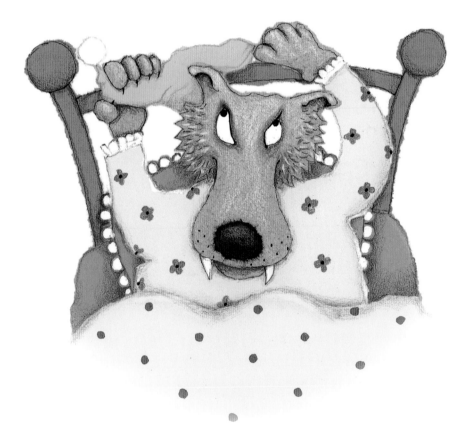

Just then, Little Red Riding Hood
knocked at the door.

"Hello Grandmother," she shouted.

"May I come in?"

"Of course, my dear," called the wolf,
licking his lips. "Come right in."

Little Red Riding Hood stared closely at the wolf.

"Oh Grandmother," she said. "What big ears you have."

"All the better to hear you with," replied the wolf.

Little Red Riding Hood edged closer.

"And what big eyes you have,"

she whispered.

"All the better to see you with," grinned the wolf.

"And what big teeth you have," exclaimed Little Red Riding Hood.

"All the better to eat you with," roared
the wolf as he jumped out of the bed.

"I don't think so," shouted Little Red
Riding Hood and raced out of the door.

A nearby woodcutter heard her cries and ran to help. He chopped off the wolf's head with his axe.

"Thank you," said Little Red
Riding Hood.

She ran to the cupboard and
let Grandmother out.
"You are a brave girl,"
said Grandmother.

"I'll never talk to strangers in the forest again!" said Little Red Riding Hood. "My mother was right. It's too dangerous!"

About the story

Little Red Riding Hood is a traditional European story, believed to be over 1000 years old. It was first published by Charles Perrault in 1697 and was later also included by the brothers Grimm in their fairy tales collections. Charles Perrault was one of the first authors to write fairy tales. He lived in Paris. He decided to write stories for children in his later life when he was 67. His most famous stories include *Little Red Riding Hood, Puss in Boots, Cinderella* and *The Sleeping Beauty.*

Be in the story!

Imagine you are Little Red Riding Hood. What will you say to your parents when you get home?

Now imagine you are Little Red Riding Hood's parents. What will you say to Little Red Riding Hood?

First published in 2014 by
Franklin Watts
338 Euston Road
London
NW1 3BH

Franklin Watts Australia
Level 17/207 Kent Street
Sydney
NSW 2000

A CIP catalogue record for this book is available
from the British Library.

The artwork for this story first appeared in
Leapfrog: Little Red Riding Hood

ISBN 978 1 4451 2839 9 (hbk)
ISBN 978 1 4451 2840 5 (pbk)
ISBN 978 1 4451 2842 9 (library ebook)
ISBN 978 1 4451 2841 2 (ebook)

Series Editor: Jackie Hamley
Series Advisor: Catherine Glavina
Series Designer: Cathryn Gilbert

Printed in China

Franklin Watts is a divison of
Hachette Children's Books,
an Hachette UK company.
www.hachette.co.uk